BEAR and SQUIRREL are FRIENDS

are FRIENDS

Yes, Really!

Deb Pilutti

A Paula Wiseman Book
Simon & Schuster Books for Young Readers
New York | London | Toronto | Sydney | New Delhi

SIMON & SCHUSTER BOOKS FOR YOUNG READERS
An imprint of Simon & Schuster Children's Publishing Division
1230 Avenue of the Americas, New York, New York 10020
Copyright © 2015 by Deb Pilutti
SIMON & SCHUSTER BOOKS FOR YOUNG READERS is a trademark of Simon & Schuster, Inc.
For information about special discounts for bulk purchases, please contact
Simon & Schuster Special Sales at 1-866-506-1949 or business@simonandschuster.com.
The Simon & Schuster Speakers Bureau can bring authors to your live event.
For more information or to book an event, contact the Simon & Schuster Speakers Bureau
at 1-866-248-3049 or visit our website at www.simonspeakers.com.
Book design by Lizzy Bromley • The text for this book is set in Garamond 3.
The illustrations for this book are rendered in gouache.
Manufactured in China • 0615 SCP
2 4 6 8 10 9 7 5 3 1
Library of Congress Cataloging-in-Publication Data
Pilutti, Deb, author, illustrator.
Bear and Squirrel are friends...yes, really! / written and illustrated by Deb Pilutti. — 1st edition.
pages cm
"A Paula Wiseman Book."
Summary: Although Squirrel's friends warn him that bears eat squirrels, and Bear's friends
remind him that squirrels make a good midnight snack, their friendship remains strong.
ISBN 978-1-4814-2913-9 (hardcover) — ISBN 978-1-4814-2914-6 (eBook)
[1. Friendship—Fiction. 2. Bears—Fiction. 3. Squirrels—Fiction. 4. Humorous stories.] I. Title.
PZ7.P6318Be 2015
[E]—dc23
2014031063

first
edition

for
Hope and Christine

It's true that Bear was much bigger than Squirrel.
And that a bear will *sometimes* eat a squirrel for dinner.
But Bear and Squirrel were friends.
They had a lot in common.

They liked to gather
acorns and blueberries.

Bear was very strong.
He would shake the trees until nuts
rained down on the forest floor.

Squirrel was very fast.
He zipped from nut to nut,
collecting them for supper.

Bear helped Squirrel make a cozy nest of leaves and twigs.

Squirrel helped Bear tidy up his den.

And they both liked to play games.

The other squirrels asked,
"Why are you hanging around with a bear?
He'll eat you up for a midnight snack."
Squirrel said, "Don't be silly!
Bear is my friend."

The other bears said, "Squirrel would
make a good midnight snack!"
Bear said, "That's ridiculous!
Squirrel is my friend."

Squirrel and Bear ignored the
other animals' remarks and
went off to play "Guess That Song."

And when Bear settled in for a long
winter nap, Squirrel waited patiently
for his friend to wake up.

And waited. . . .

And waited.

Until spring finally arrived.
Bear began to stir.

"It's good to see you," said Squirrel.

"It's good to see you too," said Bear.

"You look different," said Squirrel.

"You look different too," said Bear.

"You look delicious," said Bear.

"Why, thank you, Bear," said Squirrel.

"I mean you look like you would *taste* delicious," said Bear.

They looked at each other for a long time.

SNiff

SNiff

"I'm sorry, Squirrel, I can't help myself!" said Bear.

Excuse me!

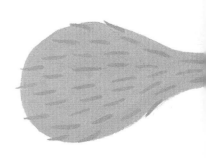

Stop, Bear!
Squirrel is your friend!

gnaw nom
CHEW
MUNCH
CRUNCH
mmmm!

But Bear couldn't stop.

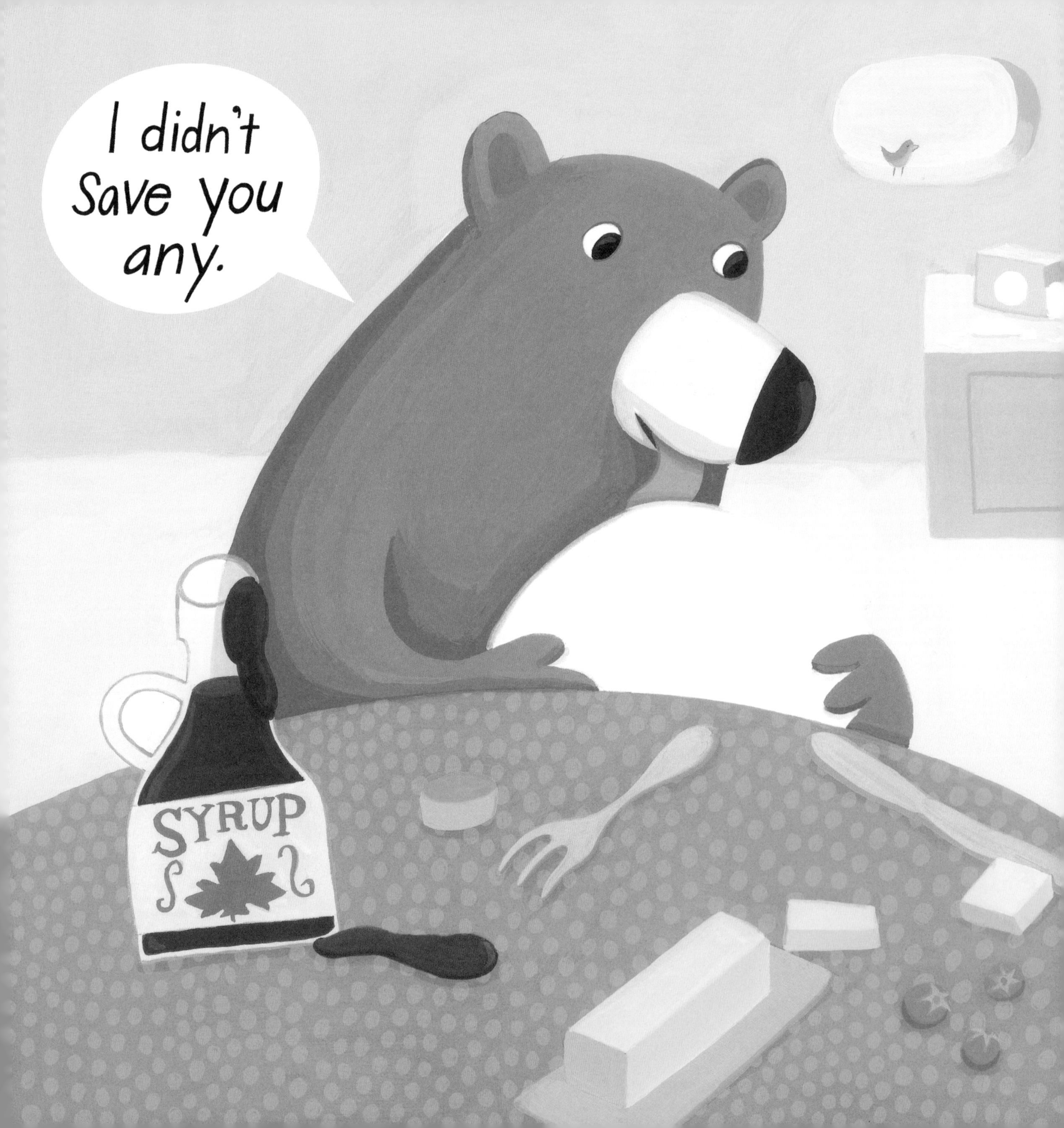
I didn't Save you any.
SYRUP

"It's okay, Bear, I can make more," said Squirrel.

Bear ate all the blueberry pancakes that Squirrel made until not a morsel was left. He ate every last berry. He even licked the plate clean.

But . . .

he did not eat Squirrel.